Alphabet Grace

Alphabet Grace

Alphabet Grace
By Meg Weidner

Printed in The United States of America
ISBN: 978-0-9826344-9-3

Sleepytown Press
www.sleepytownpress.com

I am most grateful for my darling Chickpea

Who inspires me to be more than I ever dreamt I could be

She is precocious and inquisitive

Playful, spontaneous and spunky

And just like her mother, dances pretty funky

Love Mommy M

Para mi adorado hijo Preston Santiago

!Tu eres mi inspiración y lo maravilloso de mi vida!

Te amo

Mami

Little M burst through the door, hair falling around her face
and cheeks flushed a bubbly pink.

"I love school, Grammy!"
Little M panted.
" I made new friends and sang old songs.
Mrs. Shaw says we are going to learn a lot this year,
and we are starting with the alphabet,"
Little M said.

"That is so exciting, Little M.
Would you like me to help you learn the alphabet?"
Grammy asked.

"Yea Yea Yea!!!! Please help me learn the alphabet!"

Grammy told Little M that she learned the alphabet
through a game called "Alphabet Grace."
You go through the whole alphabet in order
and say one thing you are grateful for with each letter.
Then, you make up a little rhyme so it sticks.

"Oh, Grammy, that sounds like fun!
Let's give it a try,"
Little M said.

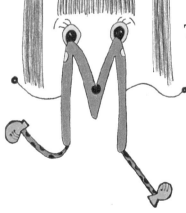

The first letter of the alphabet is 'A.'
I am grateful for"...

Aa
A is for AIRPLANES
I am grateful for airplanes

Because....
"AAAAAAAAAAAAAHHHHHHHHH"
Little M Exclaimed!
"This is so frustrating! I hate airplanes and I'm not grateful for them
and I can't make up a rhyme!"

Grammy held little M in her lap and helped her calm down.
"There are many other things that start with the letter A.
Can you think of anything else you are grateful for that starts with the letter A?"
Grammy asked.

Little M thought a minute.
"A is for Annabelle but she pulls my hair.
A is for apple but I don't eat the skin,"
Little M said.

Here Little M, Grammy said. I'll tell you what I'm grateful for."

I am grateful for my ANGEL
Who keeps the secrets that I tell.
Her wings are glittery and strong,
Definitely not flimsy.
Like you, she fills my life with joy and whimsy.

I am grateful for BUBBLES,
If they spill, no troubles.
All they are is a little soap mixed with water.
Dip the wand first
Then watch the circles swell and burst!

"Good, Little M! You got it," Grammy said.

I am grateful for CANDY
Sugar makes me feel so dandy.
Solid or striped, hard or soft,
It tastes so yummy
Going in my tummy!

I am grateful for DREAMS,
The night movies that come with chocolate moonbeams.
I close my eyes and my lids become silver screens.
Scenes start playing and stories unfold,
They seem so real and the colors are so bold!

Ee

I am grateful for ELEPHANTS
Parading for kids, ladies and gents.
They are the super stars of the traveling circus!
Good luck comes with trunks held high,
Daddy says they have great memories, I wonder why?

I am grateful for FISH
That swim in the sea and not on my dish.
They have big families just like me!
They have flashy smiles and wear big sunglasses.
They travel in schools, but do they have math classes?

I am grateful for GRAPES
On top of chocolate crepes.
Grammy gives me the fruit and the juice.
She says "it's the scoop,"
To help me poop.

I am grateful for HELP
That comes when I yelp!
Sometimes I fall down and I can't get up.
Sometimes my pants are too tight and
my zipper gets stuck.
And sometimes my laces are knotted and
my hair's all amok!

I am grateful for my IGUANA
Her name is Princess I don't wanna.
I paint her nails pink and tape bows to her head.
She makes a great pet
And even likes the vet!

I am grateful for JELL-O
The red, the green and the yellow.
It's like a magic show in my very own home.
It starts out liquid and comes out whole.
I definitely want another bowl!

I am grateful for Mommy's lips that go KISSY
She wears light lipstick so as not to be prissy.
She showers me with love after a long day at work.
She sits me on her knee
And tells me how much she loves me!

I am grateful for LAUGHTER
That makes my heart beat faster.
Sometimes I feel a tickle and start to giggle.
Sometimes it grows to a rip-roaring howl.
Oops, I wet myself! I need a towel!!!

mm

I am grateful for my hot chocolate MUG
It's warm like my Daddy's hug.
It's pink and green polka dotted-
I made it last year in school.
Art classes are totally cool!

Nn....

"Grammy, this is taking forever," Little M moaned.
Can I just skip to Z and pretend I did
N, O, P, Q, R, S, T, U, V, W, X and Y?"

"Have patience, Little M. Think of it like
a race and pace yourself.
You may just find you're sad when you get
to the end," Grammy said.

"UUUUUUUUUGGGGGHHH!
I just want to be done!!!!!"
Little M screamed.

I am grateful for NOODLES
An entire meal of noodles, the whole kit and kaboodle!
Sometimes I want Asian, sometimes Italian.
Served spicy or mild, warm or cold,
They're universal I've been told!

I am grateful for OOOHHH LA LA
It's my favorite phrase because it doesn't sound blah.
With so few words,
It says so much.
I wonder if it sounds the same in Dutch?

Pp

I am grateful for my feather PILLOW
At bed time it whispers a soft hello.
I lay down my head and sink in the middle.
It lulls me to sleep
And I dream deep, deep, deep.

I am grateful for Rosie's spinach QUESADILLA
Add some salsa and boy I feel ya!
Chop up the onions and dice up the peppers!
When served warm and cheesy,
I don't get queasy!

Rr

I am grateful for ROAD trips
Because flying makes my tummy do flips.
There is so much to do,
So much to explore
I hope Mommy and Daddy map out more!

I am grateful for SATURDAY
My one whole day to play, Play, PLAY!
I sleep in late and read books in bed.
Later my friends come over
And we play Red Rover.

Tt

I am grateful for my TREE HOUSE
It's my very own space I don't even share with a mouse.
Every corner is filled,
There is no space to waste.
I decorate it to suit MY very own taste!

I am grateful for my sassy UMBRELLA
Why? I'm gonna tell ya..
If the wind blows right
I just might fly
And on rainy days, it keeps me dry.

I am grateful for the VIOLIN
Resting on my shoulder, chin tucked in.
My bow is positioned...
The audience settles in and the lights go dim
1,2,3 Let the music begin!!!

I am grateful for Zadie's WAFFLES
They taste better than his falafel.
Syrup swims in each little square.
Every bite is so fluffy and light,
Have another one? I just might!

I am grateful for the X-RAY
That showed my insides like the light of day.
One day my tummy ached,
And it showed things our own eyes couldn't even see.
I swallowed a bug, silly me.

Yy

I am grateful for YOGA
But I don't wear a toga.
I have special pants and a fun t-shirt
with Ommmmmmm
I can do down dog, up dog, and stay in plank
And yoga has a boat pose where you just don't sank.

Grammy corrected Little M
and told her that sank should be sink.

"I'm giving myself creative liberty, Grammy.
This is America, home of the free!"
Little M exclaimed.

I am grateful for the city ZOO
On a sunny day it's a great thing to do.
Ducks quack and giraffe necks sway.
Monkeys make silly faces and lions are roaring.
Penguins waddle by and my day is far from boring!

Little M was pleased that she had learned her ABC's
and she felt quite creative making up her own rhymes.
But there was a small part of Little M that
did feel sad that the game was over.

"Sometimes beginnings are tough and the middle seems to drag.
But you only get to the end when you work hard,"
Grammy said.
"And just because you set one finish line for yourself,
it doesn't mean that there are not other races to be run."

Little M thought about it for a little while
and then had a feeling of joy come over her.
She not only learned her ABC's,
but she learned she had a lot to be grateful for, too.
And she knew there were other races to be run,
some would even have hurdles to jump.

And Little M knew just what those hurdles were...MATH!

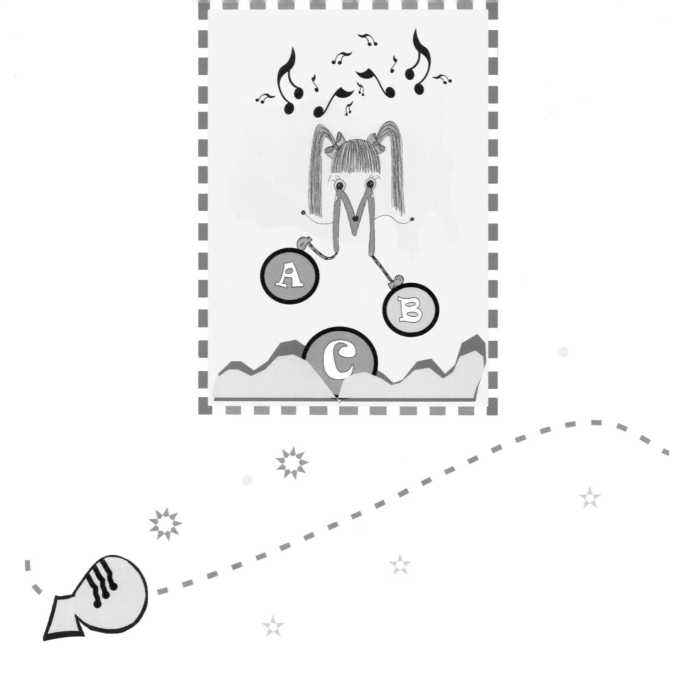

Meet the Author:

Meg Hearon Weidner is a creative artist who resides in Anniston, AL with her husband, daughter and rescue Golden. Weidner loves the arts, and is passionate about traveling, writing, and absolutely living life to its fullest. While Weidner has won awards for her short film, "You're Too," and essay "Debutante's First Bout with Poison Ivy," Alphabet Grace is the first children's story.